MONTGOMERY FANG
Professor of the Paranormal
Ghost 'n' Ghoul Hunter, Monster Catcher and
Ectoplasm Exterminator

Thursday, April 17

AN IMPORTANT WARNING TO THE READER

You are about to visit Razorback Hall, also known as the 'House of Horror'. Once the most haunted house in the country, Razorback Hall – ancestral home of the Rigsby family for over four centuries – has been free from ghosts for the past 75 years. Until a month ago, that is, when Sir Ralph became the master of the Hall.

Sir Ralph has instructed me to find out whether these new 'hauntings' are the work of genuine ghosts. There's always the possibility that they are some elaborate hoax. But for what purpose?

This is where you come in. I would take on the job myself, but I'm recovering from an attack of Swamp Fever, after tracking the infamous 'Bog Lady' to her lair . . . but that's another story.

You must go in my place. Spend this weekend at Razorback Hall and see if you can find out **who's haunting the House of Horror** . . . the living or the dead. Apart from Sir Ralph himself, all living members of the Rigsby family should be there, as well as a Colonel Bloodheart, Claptrap the butler and Mrs. Stuffing the housekeeper.

Good luck!

Montgomery Fang

P.S. You're to sleep in the Mauve Room - once said to be the most haunted room in the whole house.

WRITTEN BY
RUPERT HEATH

◆

DESIGNED BY
JOE PEDLEY

◆

PHOTOGRAPHED BY
SUE ATKINSON

◆

EDITED BY
PHIL ROXBEE COX

SERI
GA

D0682314

THERE ARE HELPFUL HINTS ON PAGE 42 AND THE ANSWERS ARE ON ...AGES 43 TO 47. ...SOLUTION TO THE ...LE MYSTERY IS ON ...E 48.

ON ECTOPLASM –
MONTGOMERY FAM...

KEEPING FIT WHILE EXORCISING

BY

MONTG...

G

Recent **RIGSBY FAMILY TREE**

SEMPER RIGSBIUS

Ebeneezer Rigsby (m. Carlotta Jones) - both deceased

Jasper Rigsby (deceased?)

Digory Rigsby (deceased)
(m. Dorcas Smith (deceased))

Regina Rigsby (deceased)
(m. Colonel W. Bloodheart)

Zelda Rigsby

Robin

Ralph

PLACEBO
PILLS
FOR FAKE
ILLS

Sir Ralph
Rigsby

NOTES

- Relatives are shown in order of age - for example, Ebeneezer's daughter Regina is older than Zelda.
- A question mark hangs over the death of Jasper Rigsby, the explorer. A crocodile wearing Jasper's old school tie was found in the deepest jungle of Mazalaland. The family believe Jasper's final journey was down the croc's throat.
- Zelda Rigsby, once known as horror-movie star Selina Stromboli, lives in Razorback Hall with only Claptrap and Mrs. Stuffing for company. In h... old age she dabbles in the supernatural, believing she can see into the future.
- The Rigsby family tradition is for the eldest male blood relative to inherit Razorback Hall.

razorback hall
by robin rigbsy
age 5

IN THE LAIR OF THE HUNTER

Time: 4pm, Thursday, April 17
Place: Professor Montgomery Fang's study

You've gone to tea with the Professor of the Paranormal
in his cobweb-covered study. He doesn't look ill.
'Master Robin will drive you down to Razorback Hall
tomorrow,' the Professor croaks, handing you piles of
papers including a set of plans. 'Sir Ralph thinks these
plans were lost,' he says, 'but they were found in a
drawer at the Hall by the butler. Keep your wits about
you when you're there. You'll need them!'

Is Sir Ralph the rightful owner of Razorback Hall?
And who is this 'Master Robin'?

PLAN OF RAZORBACK HALL

Razorback Hall
by Zelda Rigsby

PREPARATIONS

Time: 11:15am, Friday, April 18
Place: The Paranormal Emporium

Every ghosthunter needs gadgets, and you've come to the right place. This spooky store seems to sell some pretty strange things . . . and has some strange-looking customers. You're standing behind a woman wearing a long scarf, who is buying a false nose and a six-pack of rubber spiders. On *your* shopping list – written by Professor Fang – are a *SpecterScope*, some *EctoGel* and some small infrared cameras.

What do you need the infrared cameras for?

The original!
Green gel turns purple
in the presence of the
paranormal

Ectogel

TALON
TASTIES

Banish smooth
hands in a delicious
instant!

Magic Monster

Beans

Things get beastly
with a bellyful
of jelly!

Just in!
Brings out the
beast in you!

Ectogel

BAT OIL
FLY 'N' FRY

X2W339
Specterscope
Guaranteed performance.
Bulb lights up in spooky
situations

SNAKE PILLS

Charm those
snakes right out
of the trees!

Classic
Infrared Camera
'The Ghost-hunter's
invisible helper'

THINGS TO BUY
One X2W339.
I have had 100% success with this
machine in the past.
Three jars of EctoGel.
Very effective stuff.
Six X2W445s.
Set them up around the house.
Anyone crossing the infrared beam
will be photographed. Perfect for
catching fake ghosts in the night!

See you on Friday, little brother. love Ralph.

SNUG-FIT EAR PLUGS

READY TO GO

Time: 1:24pm, Friday, April 18
Place: The lobby of Robin Rigsby's apartment

You glance at the objects on Robin Rigsby's hall table while you're waiting for him to pack. You're to be driven down to Razorback Hall in the sidecar of his motorcycle. Riding on the passenger seat will be a friend of Robin's who has introduced himself as Dr. Cadmium. His hair is spiky and he keeps squinting at you through his glasses. The photo of a woman catches your eye.

Anything familiar in her picture?

Geo Collywobbles
Travel-Sick
Pills

GAMBLER'S GAZETTE
MONTHLY

You are cordially inv

A WEEKEND PA
at Razorback Ha

April 18th - April

A♥

K♣

Dear Robin,

So you're really going to do it! I
wonder if you'll have the nerve.
Here's that photo of me you asked for.
Yours forever;

Mercedes

Rigsby
rim Street

DEADWOOD & SONS
ANTIQUE FURNISHINGS
FOR RENT
R Jay Bigpress,
Razorback Hall,
Little Mulching

ITEMS DELIVERED TODAY

DELIVERY NOTE

JACK MASON
Stone and Marble
Carving a speciality
reasonable rates

ITEMS DELIVERED TODAY

R Jay Bigpress,
Razorback Hall,
Little Mulching

DELIVERY NOTE

A FOOT IN THE DOOR . . .

Time: 5:10pm, Friday, April 18
Place: The front door step, Razorback Hall

You are staring at the slippered feet of Claptrap, the butler. He's a big man, but no larger than the average truck. You've reached the house after an icy, hair-raising journey and are now waiting to come in along with the early evening mail. You can see two 'delivery notes' poking out, addressed to someone called R JAY BIGPRESS. Strange name that. Sounds like an alias . . . an anagram, perhaps?

Who might R JAY BIGPRESS be?

Uncle Frank

Aunt Matilda

The two brothers

DISASTER

DESTRUCTION

THE RED KING

To my dear Regina from Willie

Cousin Sylvester

Selina Stromboli in r first starring role

. . . AND A CHILLING PROPHECY

Time: 5:25pm, Friday, April 18
Place: The drawing room

You're shown into a chilly lamp-lit room, where an old lady sits looking at cards. 'Good evening,' she says grandly. 'I am Zelda Rigsby, and *you* should not have come. This house is cursed. The cards have predicted a horrifying accident . . . it will happen tonight!' Some of the Rigsbys in the photographs look pretty horrifying too. You think back to the names on the family tree.

Can you match the names to the faces?

DINNER IS SERVED

Time: 8:22pm, Friday, April 18
Place: The Dining Room, with the family assembled

Colonel Bloodheart has arrived in his vintage car, and you've all sat down to eat. The Colonel is on your right. He's the one with the rough hands and table manners to match. The food is strange too. Maybe that's why Robin has left the table. You're glad you brought the house plans with you. They take your mind off the meal.

Where's your bedroom on the plan?

FIGHTING SPIRIT

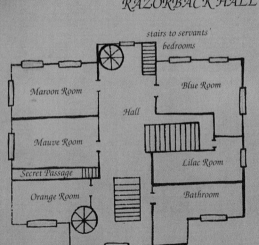

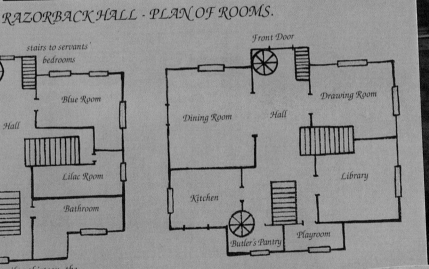

RAZORBACK HALL · PLAN OF ROOMS.

stairs to servants'
bedrooms

Front Door

Maroon Room

Blue Room

Drawing Room

Hall

Dining Room

Hall

Mauve Room

Lilac Room

Library

Secret Passage

Kitchen

Orange Room

Bathroom

Butler's Pantry

Playroom

Legend says 'when the clock strikes thirteen, the drawing room will return to how it was three hundred years ago and ghosts will rule once more'.

BLACK OUT!

Time: 8:24pm, Friday, April 18
Place: The Dining Room

Suddenly the room is plunged into darkness. You hear
a blood-curdling scream. Moments later, light is
provided by a guttering candle held by the faithful
Claptrap. A startling sight meets your eyes . . . and you
know that fakery is afoot!

But how can you be sure?

SABOTAGE!

Time: 8:31pm, Friday, April 18
Place: The Generator Room, filled with junk

You've followed the butler into the darkness. He's turned the generator back 'ON', and the power has returned. But was it a *human* hand that turned it off in the first place? You've smeared some *EctoGel* on items in this graveyard for old machinery. It's time to test for any supernatural presences.

What are the results of the EctoGel test?

THE FIEND AT THE WINDOW

Time: 1:02am, Saturday, April 19
Place: In bed, after setting up the infrared cameras
in the hall

Outside a storm is raging and you can't sleep. Suddenly
you see a terrifying figure pressed up against the
window, lit up by a tremendous flash of lightning. But,
as you stare in horror, an eerie scratching sound comes
from behind the book-lined wall to your left. You leap
out of bed to investigate the noise – leaving that creepy
monster safely locked out.

What lies behind that wall?

THROUGH THE WALL

Time: 1:05am, Saturday, April 19
Place: In the secret passage behind the bookcase

One minute you were pushing and pulling carvings on the bookcase, trying to find a lever to get you into the passage . . . the next minute the whole bookcase swung around and here you are. There aren't any ghosts or monsters around, but one of the things you *can* see might be worth a second glance. You've brought the *SpecterScope* and a flashlight along, just in case.

What suggests that someone has been in the tunnel very recently?

Interlink Rail
Slow but steady

Single journey to:
Little Mulching
FRI APRIL 18

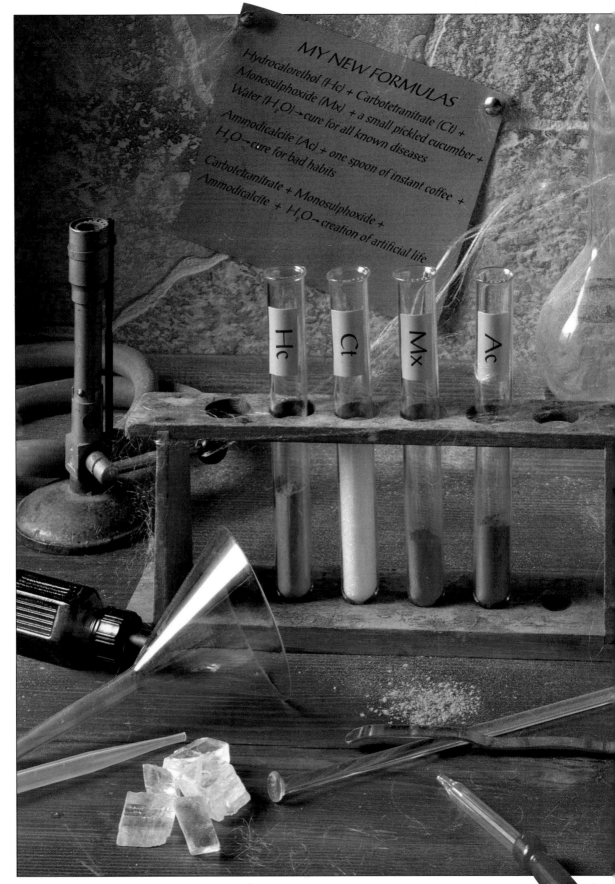

MY NEW FORMULAS

Hydrocalorethol (Hc) + Carbotetranitrate (Ct) +
Monosulphoxide (Mx) + a small pickled cucumber +
Water (H₂O)→cure for all known diseases

Ammodicalcite (Ac) + one spoon of instant coffee +
H₂O→cure for bad habits

Carbotetranitrate + Monosulphoxide +
Ammodicalcite + H₂O→creation of artificial life

INTO THE DEPTHS

Time: 1:34am, Saturday, April 19
Place: In the cellar

The secret passage has led you here, where – to your utter amazement – you find Dr. Cadmium has set up a laboratory. He's busy mixing powdered chemicals from three dishes with water in a flask marked 'X'. 'I've been experimenting down here all night,' he claims. 'This formula I'm mixing is my life's work . . . it is my life!' He laughs strangely.

Which formula is the doctor following?

A DATE WITH THE DEAD

Time: 1:50am, Saturday, April 19
Place: The family vault at the foot of the garden

Having left the cellar by a back door, you've gone outside. You investigate the light coming from the family vault, where the dead Rigsbys are normally buried. One tomb is open . . . and empty! Suddenly, a shadowy figure lunges forward, reaching for a knife. 'These are mine,' he says, pointing to some objects on the tomb. 'I'm the new gardener, MacTavish. I've been pruning by moonlight.' At the moment, you're more interested in the tomb than this odd character.

According to the inscription, who should be buried inside it? Why is that strange?

THIS MAN WAS SON OF EBENEEZER
AND LIVED HIS LIFE WITH MERIT
BUT SADLY NEVER OWNED THE HOUSE
SINCE YOUNGER SONS DON'T INHERIT

Teheiese aereme'se uepe
aenede reueneneienege,
reeeaedeye feoere oeuere
veieseieteoere teoe
feienede. Deeesetereooeye
teheiese oeneceee
yeoeue'veee reeeaede iete

IT'S ALIVE!

Time: 1:50am, Saturday, April 19
Place: The family vault at the foot of the garden

Heading back to the House of Horror, your eye is
caught by a human hand, sticking up among the flowers
. . . *with twitching fingers.* After investigation, you
discover to your amazement that the arm isn't real.
Bending closer to see what makes the fingers move, you
try to decipher the puzzling message lying in the soil.

What does it say?

BACK IN TIME?

Time: 2:29am, Saturday, April 19
Place: Outside the drawing room, looking in

With the thirteenth chime of the clock tower bell ringing in your ears, you look in through an open window at the drawing room. The room is bathed in the eerie yellow glow of the firelight . . . and the modern furniture has disappeared! You shudder. Are you witnessing the old Rigsby family legend of the room that goes back in time? Will ghosts really 'rule once more'?

Or is everything not quite what it seems?

THE COLONEL TRIPS UP

Time: 2:38am, Saturday, April 19
Place: In the hall, at the foot of the stairs

Passing through the hall, on your way to your bedroom,
you almost stumble over a body on the floor. It's
Colonel Bloodheart . . . but his groans tell you there's
life in him yet! 'This house should be mine,' he mutters.
You can see what has caused his 'accident' – a length of
green wire stretched across the floor. When he tripped
across it, the statuette fell from its heavy pedestal,
narrowly missing the colonel's head.

Have you seen that wire before?

Memorial Marrow Missing

...scandal has hit ...pped the old time ...nunity of Little ...hing as it was ...d that this ...er of the ...by

...ium Claims to Hold ...ey to Eternal Life

...l life may become more than just a dream within ...xt few years, claims eminent genetic scientist Dr. ...stopher Cadmium.

'My life's work is nearly complete,' the doctor told ...audience at the Golden Lightbulb Bright Ideas awards ...emony last week . 'I have succeeded in creating an ...ificial human who lives and breathes like you and I. ...oon the world will know my genius, and I shall be able ...o afford a new lab coat.'

Dr. Cadmium receiving a trophy at the Golden Lightbulb Bright Ideas awards ceremony

Spooky mansion good for business

The famous ghouls and ghosts of Razorback Hall have attracted many celebrities over the centuries, but none as famous as Arthur T. Bunkum, the oil millionaire, businessman and celebrity tiddlywink player. Now Mr. Bunkum has decided to go into the haunted house business himself. 'I am interested in buying Razorback Hall and turning it into a tourist attraction,' said the tycoon yesterday. Asked what price he is offering for Razorback Hall, he said: 'I won't discuss that. Let us just say that 'For the right house I would certainly go up to \$20 million. But Razorback Hall has to be proven to be haunted. I'm not investing in no fake haunted house.'

Mr Bunkum is 65.

Kid-glove Burglar Still at Large

The escaped convict ...nown as the Kid-glove ...lar is still roaming free ...Little Mulching area. ...has now kept the inhabitants of the town in a grip of fear for over four ...eeks.

Lieutenant Pigeon of the ...e Mulching police said ...'This evil must stop. ...d information about ...s gloves.'

Opposition

There are however many who oppose Dr. Cadmium's work. 'This man is evil,' says one leading critic. 'He is creating a Frankenstein's monster.' Dr. Cadmium is aware of the criticism. 'It is true that my human prototype has not been an unqualified success. He's a bit scary looking, and liable to outbursts of unpredictable violence. Still, it's just a teething problem. And, just to be on the safe side I carry my secret formula with me wherever I go,' Dr. Cadmium is a close friend of Sir Robin Rigsby, brother of Ralph, the new owner of Razorback Hall.

Stanislaus Distil Science Correspond...ent

Ghosts in the family

The recent spate of claimed hauntings at Razorback Hall, known as 'The House of Horror', is nothing new to the Rigsby family, writes Gillian Blitz. The Rigsbys have owned the spirit-infested mansion for over 400 years. In that time no less than 73 dead members of the Rigsby clan have been sighted in th... house and the grounds, som... with their heads - others n...

One of the most famous... all the Rigsby family gh... is Billy Rigsby, who... drowned by a cook in a... vat of soup in the k... kitchens in 1732. L... says that Billy now... the kitchens as a po... - a noisy, mischievo... who throws obje... creates havoc.

On other...

Cook's corner.
Sheep flu - fa...
Dog given a b...
More about t...
Prize Marr...
Cow i...os...
...ore at...

POLTERGEIST

Time: 8:30am, Saturday, April 19
Place: The kitchen

After a few hours' sleep and a quick tour of the house and gardens you've come in here for some breakfast. Everywhere else seems to be back to normal – or as normal as anything can be in the House of Horror. But someone – or *something* – has been busy in the kitchen. It looks like it's been turned inside out, and left that way. Another trick?

Which Rigsby ghost could be blamed for this havoc?

Living traditions

t is traditional for each ...
azorback Hall to take ...se...
om his father, and 'he ...
utler is no exception. ...ut ...t
Claptrap has now been at Razorback
Hall for 30 years, serving the last
three owners. 'I was named Cuthbert
after my father,' smiles Mr. Claptrap,
'so, to save confusion, I was called
'Junior' or 'JR' as a child. People
sometimes still call me JR now'.

'M...
treasure...
Rigsby, aun...
current owner, S...

Town Noticeboard

Mercedes Lustgarten
Little Mulching
Town Hall, May 17
A rare live performance
from the international
actress and comedienn...
Mercedes Lustgarten. Sh...
will perform scenes from

her film *The Nose* as w...
as her hilarious and ...
loved classic 'P...
Spider' sketch.
...e winner of the ...
...ory Rigsby memor...
...e marrow competi...
...e Stokes.

INTERESTING DEVELOPMENTS

Time: 8:30am, Saturday, April 19
Place: In Dr. Cadmium's cellar laboratory – an ideal
  photographic darkroom

Time to develop the photos from the cameras you set up
in the hallway. Each picture was taken when someone
went through one of the invisible infrared beams in the
night. Removing the photos of yourself and the colonel,
you're left with a ridiculous selection of hand-shadow
puppets! The phone rings – it's Montgomery Fang.
'How's it all going?' he asks. 'I'd love to be there, but
I've still got bat pox.' You're hardly listening. Something
is missing from the laboratory since last night . . .

What is it?

Me and Stuffing on holiday

GENERATOR ROOM

Rigsby on Top of the World

Robin Rigsby can't get enough adventure at home - so he's planning a Himalayan expedition. 'I'm trying to raise the money,' says Robin. 'My target is about $2 million.'

For Robin, whose family have owned famously haunted Razorback Hall for generations, exploring runs in the family. 'My uncle Jaspe_ was an explorer, and he fear_ nothing – except man-eat_ crocodiles. And the Yeti h_ no terrors for me. I've se_ many creepy things _ _ home to be sc_ _ _iry blob_

SOMETHING IN THE PANTRY

Time: 9:17am, Saturday, April 19
Place: The butler's pantry

While no one is around, it makes sense to have a quick peek in Claptrap's den. He's got an interesting scrapbook, full of newspaper clippings about the Rigsby family. The article about Jasper Rigsby looks particularly fascinating.

Jasper Rigsby? JR? Where have you seen those initials before?

Scaly End to an [...]

The team investigating the disappearance of Jasper Rigsby in Mazalaland have now recorded a verdict of

A crocodile yesterday

death by crocodile. 'He must have disagreed with something that ate him,' said Andrew Scroggie, one of the team. Apart from the crocodile wearing his old school tie, the only trace left of Jasper was a trunk, with the initials 'JR' on it, floating down the Umballi river.

Struck by Lightning

They say that lightning never strikes twice in the same place. That certainly isn't true in the case of Ms. Zelda Rigsby, of Razorback Hall, who was struck twice by successive bolts of lightning on her way home from shopping at Little Mulching market last Saturday. 'Mos[...] invigorating,' said M[...] Rigsby, who origin[...] struck gold as the ac[...] Selina Stromboli in [...] films as *The Beas[...]*, *Return of the C[...]* and *Vampires in the M[...]*

[...]y Firm [...]e Rocks

[...] *financial correspondent*
[...]or Electrical Co., the
[...]ge international
[...]ompany owned by Sir
Robin Rigsby, is in major
financial trouble. Recent
reports suggest that the
company has debts of up to
$10 million. Sir Ralph,
however, denied the
allegations. 'Major
Electrical is going through
a brief rough patch, it's
true, but recovery is just
around the corner.'

Prize Begonias Take Flower Show by Storm

By Our Floral Correspondent
[...]thbert Claptrap, butler at
[...]ack Hall, was today
[...] prestigious Grand
[...] Mulching
[...] for his

The Art of Shadow Puppetry

THROUGH THE KEYHOLE

Time: 11:03am, Saturday, April 19
Place: Outside the playroom, looking in through the keyhole

Passing through the hall, you've heard voices. Peeping through the keyhole in the playroom door, you see the edge of someone's blue and white apron and hear snatches of a conversation. 'You know, Cuthbert, I hope Sir Ralph is scared off. I could turn this place into a nice home for retired housekeepers if it wasn't for them Rigsbys.' You hurry away before you're caught spying.

Who is talking to whom?

TIME FOR THE TRUTH

Time: 11:44am, Saturday, April 19
Place: The library

You've summoned every suspect to the library, hoping to unmask whoever has been behind so many of these so-called supernatural happenings. While you wait for Claptrap to bring MacTavish in from the garden, a mischievous clown doll sits staring at you. Then, to your surprise, Sir Ralph himself strides into the room! He has one question on his lips. It is:

Who's haunting the House of Horror?

What do you call an annoying vampire?

A pain in the neck!

What do ghosts like to eat?

Ghoul-ash!

What's made of bread and rides a broomstick?

A sand-witch!

Why are ghosts such wimps?

They've got no guts!

How do monsters like their eggs?

Terri-fried!

Why are graveyards popular places?

People are dying to get into them!

What did the pretty ghost enter?

A boo-ty contest! (She didn't stand a ghost of a chance)

What did the grateful vampire say?

Fangs very much!

What kind of music do ghosts like these days?

Haunted House Music!

What do you call a giant monster?

... wants you to!

THE SOLUTION TO
THE WHOLE
MYSTERY IS ON
PAGE 48, BUT
DON'T CHECK IT
UNTIL YOU'RE SURE
YOU KNOW THE
ANSWER.

CONCLUSIONS

It's pretty obvious by now that one
or more people have been busy,
faking the haunting of Razorback
Hall. But why? Almost everybody in
the story has a possible motive.

The questions and clues on every
page will help you solve the mystery.
If you haven't figured it out yet, ask
yourself the following questions:

What's is familiar about the green
wire on pages 30 & 31?

Does the *appearance* of any of the
characters reveal something
interesting about their identities?

Would it have been possible for
all the 'ghostly' activity you have
witnessed to be the work of just
one person?

HELPFUL HINTS

PAGES 2 & 3
The answers to both questions lie in the family tree.

PAGES 4 & 5
Match Fang's spooky shopping list to the objects in front of you.

PAGES 6 & 7
The clue's in her clothes.

PAGES 8 & 9
Can the letters can be shuffled to form a name you've seen before? On page 2 perhaps?

PAGES 10 & 11
Think about names and name *changes*.

PAGES 12 & 13
Fang gave you the name of your room – and mentioned something else about it too.

PAGES 14 & 15
Will any of your new ghostbusting equipment help you here?

PAGES 16 & 17
The *EctoGel* is green. What does green mean?

PAGES 18 & 19
The plan of the house should come in handy.

PAGES 20 & 21
A date could be part of an important clue.

PAGES 22 & 23
Start by matching the three powdered chemicals in the dishes with those in the test tubes. Then study the formulas.

PAGES 24 & 25
The answers are in the family tree again.

PAGES 26 & 27
Try taking away some of those 'E's.

PAGES 28 & 29
Does anything label this as a set-up?

PAGES 30 & 31
You've seen a ball of green wire among someone's possessions.

PAGES 32 & 33
Find the newspaper story about a poltergeist.

PAGES 34 & 35
'X' used to mark the spot.

PAGES 36 & 37
At the 'foot' of pages 8 and 9 perhaps?

PAGES 38 & 39
Who'd want to set up a home for retired housekeepers? Where have you seen the name Cuthbert before?

PAGES 40 & 41
Have you found the answer to *every* question? If not, go through the story again before reaching your conclusion . . .

ANSWERS

PAGES 2 & 3

The notes below the tree tell you that Razorback Hall always belongs to the *eldest male blood relative* in the Rigsby family. Apart from Ralph, all the members of the Rigsby family on the tree are ruled out either because they're deceased (dead), female, non-blood relations or not the eldest. Therefore Ralph must be the rightful owner of the house.

The only other possible claimant is Jasper Rigsby. He is presumed dead by the family, but his body was never found.

If you look at the family tree on Professor Fang's desk, you'll see that Ralph's younger brother is called Robin. This must be the 'Master Robin' mentioned by Fang.

PAGES 4 & 5

You need to identify the unnamed items on Fang's shopping list. If you look at the cards by the objects on the shelves, you'll see that X2W339 is the *SpecterScope*. X2W445 is on a card by the infrared camera top left, so this must be the camera

Fang wants you to buy six of. According to his shopping list, they are 'perfect for catching fake ghosts in the night'.

PAGES 6 & 7

The distinctive green and orange scarf worn by Mercedes Lustgarten in the photograph on page 7 is the same one worn by the mysterious woman on page 4. It could well have been Mercedes in the Paranormal Emporium.

PAGES 8 & 9

The name R JAY BIGPRESS can be rearranged to make JASPER RIGSBY. We know from page 2 that this is the name of Ralph and Robin's uncle, supposedly eaten by a crocodile in Mazalaland. So who's using his name now, in such a mysterious way? And why?

PAGES 10 & 11

Uncle Frank, Aunt Matilda and Cousin Sylvester are named under their pictures. Everyone else can be identified from what you have learned about them on the family tree on page 2.

One of the figures in the photo of '*the two brothers*' is Sir Ralph Rigsby. Therefore the other must be Robin, his brother.

The man with the moustache has inscribed his picture '*To my dear Regina from Willie*'. Regina Rigsby's husband is called Colonel W. Bloodheart. The 'W' could stand for 'Willie', so this is probably the Colonel in the photo.

We know that Zelda Rigsby's movie name was Selina Stromboli. Therefore the final picture, of '*Selina Stromboli in her first starring role*', must be the young Zelda.

PAGES 12 & 13

In Professor Fang's '**AN IMPORTANT WARNING TO THE READER**' on page 1, he tells you that he's arranged for 'you to sleep in the Mauve room'. He also says that it was 'once said to be the most haunted room in the whole house.'

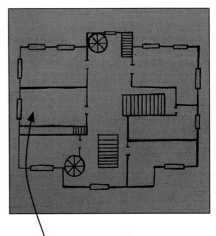

Your room is here.

Pages 14 & 15

One of your new gadgets, the *SpecterScope*, is clearly visible in the bottom left corner of page 14. On page 5, in the Paranormal Emporium, you read that the *SpecterScope* '*lights up in spooky situations*'. However, in the candle-lit dining room, the bulb on the machine is still firmly off. This helps to confirm that all these ghostly goings-on are fake.

Pages 16 & 17

EctoGel '*turns purple in the presence of the Paranormal*', according to the card in the shop on page 5. However, the *EctoGel* spread around in the Generator Room is still *green*. This indicates that nothing supernatural has happened there.

PAGES 18 & 19

Look at the plan of the house again. In one wall of the Mauve Room is a window onto the garden – this is the one that the monster is peering through. But behind the book-lined wall to your left . . . is a secret passage! This must be where the sound is coming from.

PAGES 20 & 21

The 'Interlink Rail' train ticket lying in the shadows has the date '**FRI APRIL 18**' on it. That's yesterday's date. That means that whoever dropped it has been in the passage since then.

But this raises another mystery. You, Robin and Dr. Cadmium came by motorcycle. Colonel Bloodheart came in his vintage car. Claptrap, Mrs. Stuffing and Zelda were already in the house. So who arrived by *train*?

PAGES 22 & 23

The purple mixture in the glass flask marked '**X**' is probably made up of the powdered red, white and blue chemicals beside it. The very same three chemicals are also contained in three of the test tubes in the rack on the left. They have the shortened names '**Ct**', '**Mx**' and '**Ac**'.

If you now look at Dr. Cadmium's list of '**NEW FORMULAS**', you'll see that the full names for these three chemicals are Carbotetranitrate, Monosulphoxide and Ammodicalcite. And, according to Dr. Cadmium, together with water they make a formula for the creation of artificial life!

PAGES 24 & 25

The inscription on the tomb describes the deceased as the '**SON OF EBENEEZER**'. If you refer back to the Rigsby family tree on page 2, you will see that Ebeneezer Rigsby only had two sons: Digory and Jasper. The inscription goes on to say that this tomb belongs to the '**YOUNGER SON**'. That could only mean Jasper.

But we know from page 2 that Jasper Rigsby disappeared on an expedition in Mazalaland, assumed eaten alive by a crocodile. So this tomb cannot possibly have contained the body of Jasper Rigsby, alive or dead.

PAGES 26 & 27
This note was encoded by adding the letter 'E' between every other letter. If you take away all the extra 'E's, you are left with:

This arm's up and running ready for our visitor to find. Destroy this once you've read it.

This note was clearly not intended for your eyes. It sounds more like an exchange between *accomplices*.

PAGES 28 & 29
If you look closely you will notice that the cushion on the left of the desk has a label attached to it. The label has a little picture of an antique chair on it – the same picture that appears on 'DEADWOOD & SONS' delivery note on page 8. Their business is renting antique furnishings. This is no time slip. The old furniture has been hired!

PAGES 30 & 31
There's only one place where you've seen any green wire like that before. That's on Robin Rigsby's hall table, in among his travel items.

PAGES 32 & 33
The newspaper story on page 32, entitled '**Ghosts in the Family**', mentions the ghost of Billy Rigsby, who was said to haunt the kitchen. He's supposed to be a poltergeist - a spirit who likes to make a mess. If he exists, this is just the sort of mess he might make!

PAGES 34 & 35
All the items from the night before are present and correct . . . except the beaker containing formula 'X'.

PAGES 36 & 37
The initials JR have turned up twice before in the story. First, as the monogrammed initials on Claptrap's slippers on pages 8 & 9. Second, in the

newspaper story, '**Ghosts in the Family**' on page 32, where Claptrap says: 'I was called 'Junior' or 'JR' as a child. People sometimes still call me JR now.' No connection with Jasper Rigsby there then.

PAGES 38 & 39
The speaker must be Mrs. Stuffing, the housekeeper. Who else would want the Rigsbys away from the house so she could set up a home for retired housekeepers?
    Her invisible companion is none other than Claptrap the butler. We know his first name is Cuthbert from the newspaper article '**Ghosts in the Family**' on page 32.

PAGES 40 & 41
    There are a lot of creepy things and double-dealings going on at the House of Horror. But there is only one true explanation for the 'haunting'.

You must use your detective powers of reasoning. Try to find the answers to all the questions and carefully examine all the visual clues. Then, when you are *sure* you know who's haunting the House of Horror, turn to page 48 and hold the solution up to a mirror . . .

SOLUTION

There's one thing in common with most of the 'supernatural' things you've seen at Razorback Hall. They are fakes. But who is responsible, and why? An important clue lies in the newspaper article about Arthur T. Bunkum, on page 32. He's a millionaire who's very anxious to buy a creepy old mansion, but, as he says: 'it has to be proven to be haunted. I'm not investing in no fake haunted house.'

One of the newspaper clippings in Claptrap's scrapbook on pages 36 & 37 reveals that Sir Ralph Rigsby has got BIG money problems — he needs ten million dollars immediately to save his company, the Major Electrical Co. If Sir Ralph could sell Razorback Hall to Arthur T. Bunkum, then his money problems would be over.

In the photographs of Sir Ralph on Professor Fang's desk on page 2, and with his brother Robin on pages 10 & 11, Ralph is shown wearing an unusual ring with a red stone. The same ring appears on the hand of MacTavish, the strange 'new gardener', you met by the tomb on pages 24 & 25. One of the keys on MacTavish's key ring matches one in Claptrap's pantry tagged 'Generator Room.' This was the key Sir Ralph, disguised as MacTavish, used to get into the generator room to switch the power off during dinner on pages 12 & 13. Sir Ralph had come down, in disguise, by train — dropping his ticket in the secret passage on page 20.

Ralph needed someone to confirm that the house really was haunted again . . . that's where you fitted in. If he could trick you into believing that the hauntings were genuine, then Arthur T. Bunkum might buy the house. No wonder Sir Ralph was so eager to plant the idea that his uncle, Jasper Rigsby, had come back from the dead by faking an open tomb on pages 24 & 25 — don't forget the delivery note from Jack Mason ('marble carving a speciality') on page 8.

But that's not the whole story. He must have had help. When he was in the secret passage, someone had to be at the window on pages 18 & 19. The note left beside the mechanical arm was from one schemer to another. Then there was all that rented antique furniture. Ralph couldn't have moved it all into place without the help of . . . his brother, Robin. He was the one who had left the dining table just before the power was switched off. He was the one controlling the dinner-time 'ghosts'.

Think back to that green wire stretched across the hall floor, which tripped Colonel Bloodheart up. It came from the ball of wire on Robin's lobby table on page 7. Robin needed money too, to fund his trip to the Himalayas. If Arthur T. Bunkum bought Razorback Hall, both brothers would get what they want. Ralph and Robin haunted the 'House of Horror.'

But they needn't have bothered. The bulb on the SpecterScope is lit up for the first and only time in the kitchen on pages 32 and 33, which means that there was genuine paranormal activity at work in the room. Billy Rigsby, the family poltergeist, is back in action . . . perhaps Arthur T. Bunkum will buy the house after all!

First published in 1996 by Usborne Publishing Limited, Usborne House, 83-85 Saffron Hill, London EC1N 8RT, England.
© Copyright 1996 Usborne Publishing Ltd.
The name Usborne and the device 🐝 are Trade marks of Usborne Publishing Ltd. All rights reserved.
Printed in Spain   U.E. First published in America March 1997.